Contents

Writer: Michael Butcher

Artwork: RWS Graphics

Copyright © 1991 Thames Television Plc
All rights reserved. Published in Great Britain by
World International Publishing Limited,
an Egmont Company, Egmont House, PO Box 111,
Great Ducie Street, Manchester M60 3BL.
Printed In Italy.
ISBN 0 7498 0266 9

In Disguise

ippy is looking through a box of **isguises**. "No one will be able to uess who I am if I wear this," he huckles.

Zippy puts on the disguise. "Hello, Mr Bear!" he says to Bungle in a funny voice. "Oh, hello, Zippy," says Bungle.

Humph! How did he recognise ne?" complains Zippy. He goes ack to the box to see if he can nd a better disguise.

"Hello, Zippy," says George when he sees his friend. "Why are you wearing that hat and scarf? Are you feeling cold?"

5

"There must be a good disguise in here," says Zippy, looking through the box again. "This **mask** should fool someone!"

"Hello, Geoffrey! **GRRR**!" Zippy growls in his scariest monster voice. "Ha, ha! I recognise that zip!" laughs Geoffrey.

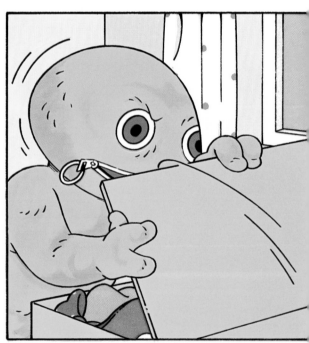

"Oh, no!" groans Zippy, taking off the mask. "I just can't find a disguise that works!" He hurries back upstairs.

"These silly disguises are no use at all," Zippy moans, putting them back in the box. "They're a load of rubbish!"

Just then, Geoffrey, George and Bungle come into the room. "Oh, Geoffrey!" gasps Bungle. "Who's that over there?"

"Ah-ha!" laughs Zippy. "So I have managed to fool you with one of my brilliant disguises! It's me . . . **Zippy**! Ha, ha!"

Hey! Wait a minute!" Zippy says, suddenly. "I'm not even wearing a disguise now. I've put them all away!"

"Now you mention it, I think I do recognise you, Zippy," chuckles Bungle. "**Huh**! What a silly joke!" puffs Zippy.

A Dotty Drawing

Bungle is drawing a picture of something Geoffrey always takes on holiday with him. Can you guess what it is? You can help Bungle finish his drawing by joining the dots. Then you can colour it in, too.

Answer: Bungle is drawing a camera.

Make A Bird-feeder

George likes feeding the birds out in the Rainbow garden, so Geoffrey is showing him how to make a special **bird-feeder**.

You can make one, too. It's very easy and all you need is a plastic egg box, a large needle, string and some bird food.

1. Geoffrey takes the bottom half of the egg box and makes a small hole in the middle of each side with the large needle. (You will need to ask a grown-up to do this for you.)

2. George threads string through each hole and Geoffrey helps him tie it securely. Then they knot all four pieces of string together over the box and tie another piece to the knot to hold the bird-feeder up.

3. Now George puts bird food in the egg box sections. He uses breadcrumbs, suet, nuts and raisins. He also fills one of the sections with water for the birds to drink.

4. Finally, Geoffrey hangs up the full bird-feeder from a tree in the Rainbow garden. (If you have nowhere to hang your bird-feeder you could just put it on a window-sill.)

The Breakdown

"Oh, dear! I can't put this silly thing on right," moans Bungle. "Do I really have to wear a tie, Geoffrey?"

"Well, I would like you to look smart this evening," Geoffrey says, helping Bungle to put his tie on. "We've all been invited to dinner with my friends, Dawn and Andrew. George and Zippy are wearing shirts and ties."

"But **we're** ready to go, Geoffrey!" calls Zippy, from downstairs. "Not like that **slowcoach**, Bungle!"

"Have you had a wash yet, Zippy?" asks Geoffrey.

"Er, well . . . no," stutters Zippy. "I was . . . er . . . just about to have a wash." He rushes up to the bathroom before Geoffrey can say a word!

At last, everyone is ready, so they climb into Geoffrey's car and set off. "Is it far to Dawn and Andrew's house?" asks George. "I hope we won't be late."

"I just hope we get there in time for dinner!" says Zippy. **"I'm hungry!"**

Suddenly, they all hear a loud **bang**! "What was that?" gasps Bungle in surprise. Geoffrey stops the car right away and gets out to have a look.

"Oh, no!" he groans. "We've got a **flat tyre**. I must have driven over something sharp."

"Can you fix it, Geoffrey?" asks Bungle. "Or will we need a new car?"

"Don't worry, Bungle," says Geoffrey, opening the car boot. "I can't mend the flat tyre, but I can swap the wheel for the spare one in here." He takes the spare out of the boot and puts it next to the car.

"Now where did I put the **jack**?" Geoffrey mutters to himself.

"Who's Jack?" wonders George. "Is he going to help you put the spare wheel on, Geoffrey?"

"I suppose he is in a way, George," laughs Geoffrey. "But this jack isn't a person, it's a tool I can use to help me lift the car up a little while I change the wheel."

"I hope that this isn't going to take too long," Zippy complains. "Our dinner will be ready soon and we won't be there in time to have it if we don't hurry up!"

"Give me a chance, Zippy!" says Geoffrey. "I'm doing this as fast as I can." He uses the jack to lift the car up a little and then starts undoing the nuts holding the wheel on. Finally, Geoffrey manages to get the wheel with the flat tyre off. "**Phew**! Half-way there!" he puffs.

"Is there anything we can do to help you?" Bungle asks Geoffrey.

"No, thanks, Bungle!" gasps Geoffrey, as he struggles to put the spare wheel on. "Just keep a safe distance away from the car, please. I've nearly finished now." Geoffrey tightens up the nuts to hold the wheel firmly in place while the others watch. Finally, he lets the car down again with the jack and puts all his tools back in the boot.

"Will the car be all right now?" asks George.

"I think so," nods Geoffrey, "but I'll have to get the flat tyre mended at the garage in the morning."

"What are we waiting for then?" asks Zippy, jumping back inside the car. "Let's get going, Geoffrey! Dinner's getting cold!" The others get in the car, too, and Geoffrey starts it up again.

It is not long before they arrive at Dawn and Andrew's house. Geoffrey parks the car and they all get out. "I'll ring their bell," says Bungle, rushing up to Dawn and Andrew's front door.

"Oh, hello, Bungle!" smiles Andrew, opening the door. "We were wondering what had happened to you. Come in!"

"I'm sorry we're late, Andrew," says Geoffrey, as they go in. "We had a bit of trouble with the car . . ."

"Never mind," says Dawn. "You're here now and, my goodness, aren't Bungle, George and Zippy looking **smart** this evening? They're smarter than you, Geoffrey!" she giggles.

"What do you mean, Dawn?" puzzles Geoffrey. "I'm wearing my best shirt . . . **oh, no**!" he groans, realising that he is all messy from changing the wheel on the car.

"I think you'd better go and have a wash before you have your dinner, Geoffrey!" Zippy tells him.

"I think you're right, Zippy," Geoffrey sighs. "I'll have to get washed and cleaned up all over again!"

Bungle's Photo Album

Lots of you send us photographs of yourselves and Bungle likes to keep them all in a special photo album. Here are some of his favourite photographs . . .

 This is Matthew Barnard with a very good friend of his! Matthew comes from Bromley.

Abigail Stubbs of Peterborough loves animals! Here she is visiting London Zoo.

 Caroline Stephens lives in London and Rainbow is her favourite comic!

Look at this super Zippy puppet! Rachel Collins of New Eltham made it with a little bit of help from her daddy!

Claudia Matilda Bagley and her brother, Oliver, of Lowestoft are both great fans of Rainbow!

Isn't Rebecca Souter's rainbow duvet cover smashing? She comes from Lymm.

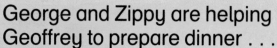

George and Zippy are helping Geoffrey to prepare dinner . . .

NO WAY OUT

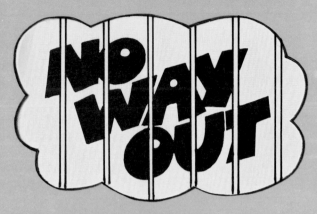

Hey, Zippy! What room has no doors or windows?

That's silly, George! You couldn't get in or out of it!

There's no such thing as a room with no doors or windows!

Yes, there is . . . a **mushroom**! Ha, ha, ha!

Oh, no!

Geoffrey's Big Red Ladder

Here's my big red ladder.
Doesn't it look tall?

Standing here beside it,
I start to feel quite small!

I sometimes climb
up to the top,
And take a look
around . . .

But I always
feel much safer,
With my two feet
on the ground!

17

Rainbow Storytime
Titch's Lasso Lesson

One morning, as Titch the Mouse was eating his breakfast, he heard a knock at his little mouse door.

"I wonder who that could be at this time of the day?" thought Titch. He hurried over and opened the door.

"Howdy, Titch!" said Elmer, walking into Titch's mousehole. "I've come to give you a **lasso lesson**." Elmer was Titch's cowboy cousin and he loved to show off all the tricks he could do with his lasso.

"A lasso lesson?" puzzled Titch, scratching his head. "Why should I want a lasso lesson, Elmer? I don't even have a lasso!"

"Don't worry, Titch," smiled Elmer, handing his cousin a lasso. "You can borrow my spare one."

"But, Elmer, I don't really need a lasso, thank you very much," said Titch. "I'm not a cowboy mouse like you."

"Ha, ha!" laughed Elmer. "If you **were** a cowboy mouse, then you wouldn't need lasso lessons, would you? Come on, I have a

lot to teach you." With that, Elmer took Titch out of his mousehole and over to a big table in the kitchen.

"First of all, I'll teach you how to lasso a piece of cheese that is hard to reach in any other way," Elmer told Titch. "Can you see any cheese up on that table?"

"I certainly can!" grinned Titch, licking his lips. "Perhaps lassoes are useful after all!" Titch liked anything that helped him get his little mouse hands on cheese!

"All right then, Titch," said Elmer. "Start twirling your lasso slowly above your head . . ."

Titch tried to do exactly what Elmer told him to, but instead of lassoing the cheese, he lassoed a nearby pepperpot and knocked it over!

"Look out, Elmer!" cried Titch, as a cloud of pepper floated down on the two mice. "**ATT-CHOO**!" sneezed Titch.

Titch and Elmer scampered back to Titch's mousehole to get away from the pepper storm! "I'm sorry about that, Elmer," spluttered Titch. "I don't think I've got the hang of using a lasso yet, have I?"

"Not yet," smiled Elmer, shaking his head. "It looks like you're going to need quite a few more lessons, doesn't it?"

Snow Fun!

Geoffrey has brought his friends to the park to play in the snow. Bungle and Zippy are busy building snowmen, while George is having a ride on his sledge. If you look carefully, you will see that there are six very strange things going on in the park today. Can you spot them all?

21

The Great Georgio's Hat Trick

George is pretending to be **The Great Georgio** ... the world's greatest magician! "Look at this!" he tells his friends.

"I am going to eat this sweet and then use my magic to make it appear **underneath** one of these hats," he explains.

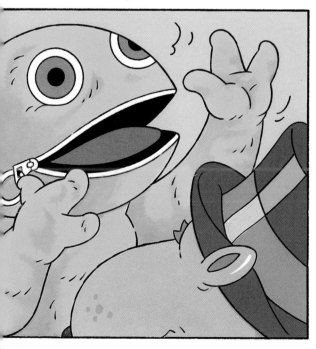

"**Ha, ha**! But that's impossible!" laughs Zippy. "Once you've eaten the sweet it will be gone. It won't be under a hat!"

"We will see, Zippy," grins The Great Georgio, unwrapping the sweet and eating it. "Now choose a hat!" he continues.

"This is silly!" scoffs Zippy. "You pick one, Bungle." "All right then, Zippy," Bungle says. "I'll choose that one!"

The Great Georgio takes off his hat and picks up the one Bungle has chosen. "**Hey**! What are you doing now?" asks Zippy.

"I'm putting this hat on," The Great Georgio tells him. "I told you that the sweet would be underneath it, didn't I?"

"Well, now it is!" he goes on. "The hat is on my head and the sweet is underneath it in my tummy!" The others just groan!

A Fishy Race

This is a funny game that Bungle, George and Zippy love to play at parties. It's very easy to make and play and you can have as many players as you want. All you need is a sheet of paper and a rolled up newspaper for each player, crayons or felt pens and a pair of round-ended scissors.

First, draw a simple fish shape on a piece of paper like the one below (make your fish about 20cm long). Then cut it out. You can draw an eye on it, or colour it as brightly as you like. You will need to make a fish for each player.

Now line up the fish at one end of a room, in front of the players. Everyone has a rolled up newspaper and, on the word "GO!", they have to whack the ground with it to make their fish fly forward. They keep on doing this until someone's fish reaches the other end of the room and wins the race!

A Donkey's Tail

"**Found you, Zippy**!" shouts Bungle. He is playing hide and seek with his friends up in their bedroom. "Now I wonder where George could be?"

"He's hiding under the bed," Zippy tells Bungle.

"**Hey**! That's not fair!" says George, popping out from underneath the bed. "You're not meant to tell Bungle where I am just because he's already found you."

"Oh, this is a silly game anyway," complains Zippy. "There must be something better that we can play."

"How about **stick-the-tail-on-the-donkey**?" suggests Bungle.

"I don't know that game, Bungle. Will we need a **real** donkey?" asks George. "I don't think Geoffrey will let us bring a donkey into our bedroom!"

"**Ha, ha**! Silly Georgy-Porgy!" laughs Zippy. "You don't need a real donkey to play a game of stick-the-tail-on-the-donkey . . . er, do you, Bungle?"

"Of course not," grins Bungle. He fetches a large rolled up piece of paper from the toy cupboard. When he unrolls it, the others see that it is a big picture of a donkey . . . **without a tail**! "Now all we need is a tail for the donkey, some sticky tape and a blindfold."

They soon find what they need and Bungle sticks the picture of the donkey to the bedroom door. "What do we have to do now?" George asks.

"You have to wear the blindfold and then try to stick the donkey's tail onto the picture as close to the right place as you can," explains Bungle. He puts the blindfold around George's eyes and lets him have a go.

"This is very hard, Bungle," says George, sticking the tail onto one of the donkey's legs! It is Bungle's turn next, but he sticks the tail on the poor donkey's head!

"Hee, hee! You're not much good at this game, are you, Bungle?" chuckles Zippy.

"**Huh**!" snorts Bungle. "You have a try then, Zippy! We'll see how you get on." Bungle

puts the blindfold on Zippy and gives him the donkey's tail.

"Oh, dear," thinks Zippy. "I can't see a thing with this blindfold on. Perhaps if I peek just a little . . ." He quickly pulls the blindfold down a bit, so he can see the donkey. Then he pulls it back over his eyes before Bungle and George can see him cheating. Hmm, Zippy thinks, I have to hurry over and stick this tail on the donkey, while I can still remember the right place . . .

But as Zippy rushes over to the bedroom door, Geoffrey opens it from the outside!

"**Oof**!" cries Geoffrey, as Zippy runs into him and sticks the donkey's tail on his nose! "What's going on?" Geoffrey wants to know.

"We're playing a game of stick-the-tail-on-the-donkey," Bungle explains. "It looks like Zippy thinks you are the donkey, Geoffrey!" he giggles.

"Oh, dear," blushes Zippy when he takes off the blindfold and sees what he has done. "You do look funny with a donkey's tail stuck to your nose, Geoffrey!"

Bungle and George can't help laughing!

George's Garden-word

You might find any of the creatures on this page in a garden. See if you can help George fill their names in on the crossword below.

1 across

1 down

3 across

2 down

6 across

4 across

5 down

Answers:

Attack Of
The Banana Monster!

"Rod, Jane and Freddy want me to play a part in one of their shows," Geoffrey tells George. "These are my words here . . ."

"**Look out**!" George cries out suddenly, as Bungle throws a ba to him. Poor Geoffrey has to duc out of the way!

"Please stop messing around, Bungle," Geoffrey tells him. "I'm trying to learn my words for my part in this play."

Zippy comes over to see what i happening. "Do you have to mak so much noise eating th banana?" Geoffrey asks him.

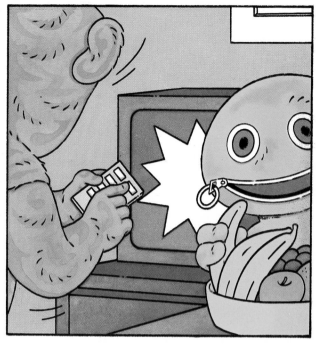

Never mind," smiles Geoffrey. "I now I won't get any peace and quiet in here, so I'll go upstairs to earn my words."

When Geoffrey has gone, Zippy decides to help himself to another banana! "I wonder what is on the TV?" says Bungle.

When Bungle turns the TV on, he sees that a funny monster film is on. "**Oh-ho**! Look at this, Zippy!" e laughs.

"There's a **giant pineapple** on the loose. It's chasing after people!" says Bungle. "What a silly film!" laughs Zippy.

"You wouldn't think it was silly if there was a giant pineapple coming to get **you**, Zippy!" George tells him.

"Silly Georgy-Porgy!" laughs Zippy. "It's only a film, you know. There's no such thing as a red pineapple monster!"

Just then, there is a funny noise out in the hall. "What could that be?" asks Bungle. "I'd better go and see!"

Bungle goes out to the hall, but he soon rushes back in. "**Help**!" he cries. "There's a big **banana monster** out there!"

Ha, ha! You can't trick **me**, Bungle-Bonce!" laughs Zippy. "There's no such thing as a banana monster either . . ."

"**AGGHH**!" cries Zippy, as he opens the door. "There really **is** a banana monster! It's come to get us! **Help! Help**!"

UMF! UMF!" moans the banana monster as it staggers into the room. "Quick! Let's hide behind here!" says Bungle.

They all hide behind the sofa. "What are we going to do now?" Zippy worries. "The monster will soon find us here!"

Then George notices something on the banana monster. "That's funny," he thinks. "I wonder why it has a zip on its head?"

George goes over to the banana monster to unzip the zip. "Oh, be careful, George!" Bungle warns. "Don't let it get you!"

Bungle can hardly believe it as the giant banana takes its head off! "Thanks, George," says Geoffrey. "I was **stuck**!"

"Do you like my costume for Rod, Jane and Freddy's play?" asks Geoffrey. "It didn't fool me at all!" insists Zippy!

The Monster In The Milk!

Here's how you can make your very own banana monster milk drink!

What you need:
a glass of milk, a banana, flaked almonds, some small sweets

What you do:
1. Peel the banana and cut off one end with a round-ended knife.

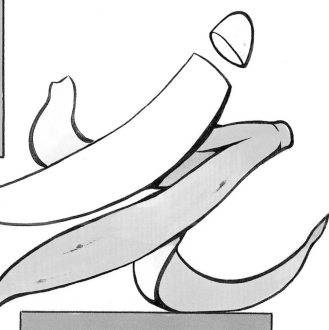

2. Very carefully cut a mouth-shaped slit in the other end of the banana like this.

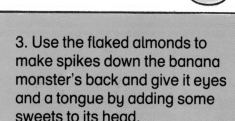

3. Use the flaked almonds to make spikes down the banana monster's back and give it eyes and a tongue by adding some sweets to its head.

4. Stand the banana in the glass of milk so that its 'head' sticks out!

Now your monster milk is ready to drink!

Rainbow Storytime
Lost In The Woods

Suzy lived in a big town, but she loved staying with her grandmother out in the country.

"There are so many wonderful things to see around here," Suzy smiled, when she was visiting her grandmother one weekend. Suzy loved all the pretty flowers and the tall trees she could find in the country, but most of all she loved Toby . . . her grandmother's little dog!

"Come on, Toby!" she called, later on. "Let's go for a walk." Toby wagged his tail happily. He liked it when Suzy took him for walks.

"Don't go too far, Suzy!" warned her grandmother. "It's easy to get lost in the woods, you know. And dinner will soon be ready, so please don't be long."

Suzy promised to hurry back and then she and Toby set off for their walk. Suzy decided to count how many different kinds of flowers she could see as she went, but she soon lost count!

"Ooh, look at that pretty butterfly over there, Toby!" said Suzy, a little later. Then she realised that Toby had disappeared! "**Toby**! Where are you?" she called, but there was no sign of him.

"Oh, dear," worried Suzy. "He must be lost in the woods! What am I going to do now? Grandmother is expecting us back very soon for our dinner. I have to find him." She wandered further and further into the woods, calling out Toby's name, but the little dog was nowhere to be found.

"I'm not even sure if I know my own way back now," Suzy sobbed. Then she heard her grandmother's voice from a long way behind her.

"Suzy! Are you all right?" she was calling from the edge of the woods. Suzy rushed back to her grandmother and told her that Toby was lost in the woods.

"No, he's not!" laughed Suzy's grandmother, as Toby rushed out of her house, licking his lips. "He came back here ahead of you because he knew it was dinner time for **him** as well!"

"Oh, you greedy thing, Toby!" smiled Suzy. "So you weren't lost after all . . . you were just very **hungry**!"

The Pop Concert

Your Rainbow friends would love to be in a famous pop group. This is what they think it would be like if they could play at a real pop concert. Do you know what they have called their pop group? (It is written on their big drum!)

How many **drums** can you count in this picture?

How many **scarves**? How many **caps**?

How many **guitars**? How many **flags**?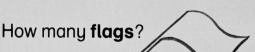

TALKING FRUIT

Can I borrow your banana for a minute, Bungle?

I suppose so . . . but **don't** eat it!

What did one banana say to the other banana?

I don't know. What did it say?

Nothing at all! Bananas can't speak . . .

. . . but they **do** taste very nice! **Hee, hee**!

The Great Georgio's Magic Page

The Great Georgio is back with another amazing magic trick for you to try on your friends. All you need is a sheet of paper and a large tin of fruit or baked beans.

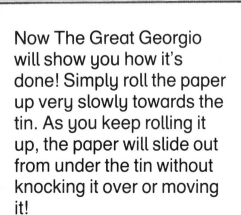

First place the tin on the sheet of paper on the floor. Then ask your friends to remove the paper **without** touching or moving the tin. They may try to pull the paper out very quickly, but it won't work. Eventually, they are sure to give up.

Now The Great Georgio will show you how it's done! Simply roll the paper up very slowly towards the tin. As you keep rolling it up, the paper will slide out from under the tin without knocking it over or moving it!

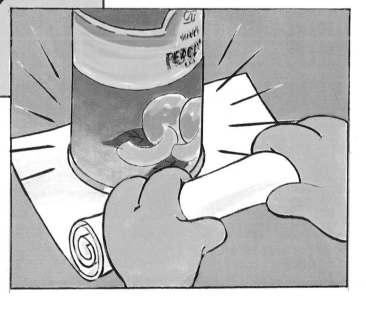

Down On The Farm

Geoffrey, Bungle, George and Zippy are visiting a **farm** in the country.

"My friend, Greg, is the farmer here," Geoffrey tells his friends. "He said we could have a good look around the place. I wonder where he is?"

"Oh, dear! Look at that, Geoffrey!" cries George, pointing at something in a nearby field. "That horrible dog is scaring those poor sheep over there. It's chasing them all over the place! We have to stop it!"

"**Ah-ha**!" smiles Geoffrey. "I think you may have found the farmer, George. Let's go and see." Geoffrey leads the way over to where George was pointing.

"But what about the poor sheep, Geoffrey?" worries Bungle. "The dog is still chasing them around. I can see it now, too."

"It's all right, Bungle," Geoffrey says, as they walk into the field and see the farmer. "The dog isn't trying to scare the sheep. It's just helping the farmer to herd them into their **pen** . . ."

"**Ha**! That's very silly, that is, Geoffrey!" scoffs Zippy, holding up a writing pen. "You'd never fit all those big sheep in a little pen!"

"I didn't mean a writing pen, Zippy," Geoffrey laughs. "The farmer wants the sheep to go into a **sheep pen**. That's a small fenced off area where they will be kept for a while." Geoffrey points to the sheep, just as they race into the sheep pen and the farmer closes the gate behind them.

"Hello, Geoffrey!" calls the farmer. "I'm glad you could come. Sorry I wasn't there to meet you, but I just needed to get these sheep rounded up."

"That's all right, Greg," says Geoffrey. "I know that the farm keeps you very busy. It was nice of you to ask us to come and look around." He introduces Bungle, George and Zippy to the farmer.

"Well, I'm pleased to meet you all," smiles Greg. "Now, what would you like to see first?"

"Have you got any **chickens**?" Zippy asks. "Chickens are funny animals. They run around going **CLUCK! CLUCK! CLUCK!** all the time!" Greg takes them all to see his chickens. He even gives them some eggs to take home with them when they go.

Next they visit some cows in a big barn. "We get all our milk from cows like these," explains Geoffrey. Then the farmer shows Bungle, George and Zippy a very big work horse and finally they visit some pigs in their pigsty.

"It must be lovely to be a farmer," says George. "I wish I could be one. I'd like to live in the country with all those nice animals."

"Well, it is very hard work, too, George," Greg tells him, "but I enjoy it."

"I don't think **I'd** like to be a farmer," says Zippy. "I wouldn't like to have to do **too much** hard work!"

"Ah," grins the farmer, "then I think I know just the farm for you, Zippy." He takes Zippy and the others into his farm house and gives them a big cardboard box.

"What's this?" puzzles Zippy.

"Open it and you'll find out!" says Greg. Zippy opens the box and finds lots of toy farm animals and buildings inside it.

"Look, it's a **toy farm**!" announces Zippy, as he empties all the pieces onto the floor. Bungle and George help him set up the farm and they are soon busy playing with it.

"That should keep them quiet for a while," Greg says to Geoffrey. "I'll make you all something to eat now." The farmer soon makes a big plate of sandwiches for his friends.

"**Bungle! George! Zippy!**" calls Geoffrey. "Greg has made us all some sandwiches.

Come on!" But they are so busy playing with the toy farm that they don't hear him!

"I know what to do," smiles Greg. He whistles to his dog and it rushes through to the other room.

The dog barks at Bungle, George and Zippy. "Ooh, I wonder what it wants?" says George. "Perhaps we'd better go and ask the farmer." They follow the dog to where Geoffrey, Greg and all the sandwiches are.

"**Ha, ha**! That worked well, Greg," laughs Geoffrey. "Your dog is just as good at rounding up Bungle, George and Zippy as it is sheep!"

The Lost Bananas

Zippy has hidden away a secret supply of bananas, but now he is feeling hungry and he can't remember where they are! Can you help him find his way through this maze to his bananas?

Bowled Over

Geoffrey has brought his friends to a special place to play **ten-pin bowling**. "It's a bit like skittles," he tells them.

"You have to roll a ball down there and try to knock the **pins** over," Geoffrey explains. "This ball is heavy!" gasps George.

"That one is far too big for you, George," Geoffrey laughs. He gives George a much lighter bowling ball to use.

George rolls the ball all the way down the bowling alley and he manages to knock down three pins. He is very pleased.

"Well done," Geoffrey says to George. "That was very good for your first try." "**I'll** do even better!" boasts Bungle.

Bungle takes a big swing and rolls his bowling ball as hard as he can. "**Oh, no**!" he groans. "It's fallen into the ditch!"

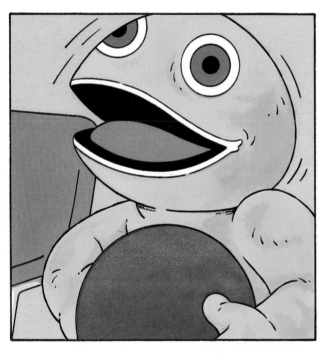

"Ha, ha! Trust Bungle-Bonce to miss the pins altogether," laughs Zippy, getting ready to have a go himself.

"**Hooray**!" shouts Zippy, as his bowling ball knocks down **six** pins. "Here, Bungle," Geoffrey smiles. "Have another go."

"If I roll the ball very hard, I should easily knock some of the pins over this time," says Bungle. "Here goes . . . **OOPS**!"

"Have another try," suggests Geoffrey. "Oh, I'm fed up with this," moans Bungle, rolling a ball slowly up the alley . . .

Bungle doesn't even watch as his bowling ball gently hits the pins in just the right place to knock them all over!

Bungle can hardly believe his luck. "Sometimes it is a good idea not to try **too hard** in this game!" laughs Geoffrey.

ART GALLERY

You send in lots and lots of fantastic pictures to our comic every week. Here are just a few of the very best ones . . .

Lucy of Newcastle in Staffordshire drew this colourful picture of Bungle, George and Zippy!

This lovely picture of George is by Robyn Keep of Maidstone!

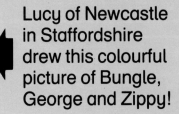

Russell Williamson of Shepherdswell has sent us this smashing picture of his Rainbow friends!

Doesn't Bungle look smart in this picture by Daniela and Sara Felice?

Becky Joy of Staplehurst did this super drawing of Bungle, Geoffrey, George and Zippy!

Bungle

George

Geoffrey

Zippy

Here's Zippy, as drawn by Gemma Williams of Crawley!

51

Rainbow Storytime
Out In The Open

CRASH! BANG! WHACK! "Oh, what a terrible noise!" groaned Archie the spider. Archie lived in a web high up in a cinema and this week they were showing a very noisy film. Poor Archie just couldn't get to sleep, however hard he tried!

"This is no good at all," yawned the very tired spider. "I'm going to have to make myself a new web **outside** the cinema . . . away from all these bangs and crashes!" Archie crept down from his web and slipped outside through a little crack in the wall that he knew.

"Ah, that's better," smiled Archie, looking around for a good spot to make a web. "Let me see now . . . that fence over there looks quite peaceful." So he set to work spinning a brand-new web, well away from the noisy cinema!

"**Phew**!" gasped Archie, a while later. "Finished at last! Building webs is hard work, but it will be worth it if I get a good night's rest now." He settled down in his nice new web and sighed happily. Then he felt a spot of rain on his head. Soon it was raining quite heavily!

"Oh, no!" groaned the poor wet spider. "This is nearly as bad as being inside the cinema. Even my web is wet through . . . **ARRGGHH**!" Archie's web was so wet that he slipped right off it!

"**Ouch**!" cried Archie, as he hit the ground. "That hurt!" He picked himself up again and slowly climbed back up to his web. But, no matter how hard he tried, Archie just couldn't get comfortable again in the slippery wet web!

"I have to get out of this pouring rain," he said, "but I can only think of one place to go." Archie made his way miserably over to the crack in the wall of the cinema and crept back inside. To his surprise, however, there were no loud noises to be heard!

"What can have happened?" thought Archie. Then he noticed that the whole place was empty. "Where have all the people gone?" he frowned. Then Archie started laughing. "Of course!" he chuckled. "The film has **finished**! It must have ended while I was outside." Everything was quiet inside the cinema because it was closed for the night!

"Ah, it's good to be home **and** dry," smiled Archie, racing up to his old web and going straight to sleep!

Zippy's Favourite Food

Of all the things I like to eat,
What's my favourite, have you guessed?
There's cheese and jam and apple pie,
But bananas are the best!

It is breakfast time in the Rainbow House. "Hurry up, Geoffrey!" says Zippy. "We're **very** hungry."

Just then, George hears a noise from the front door. "I'll go and see what it is," says Zippy.

"But your breakfast is ready," says Geoffrey. "This is better than breakfast," Zippy calls out.

"This week's **Rainbow Comic** has just arrived," grins Zippy. Bungle and George want to read it, too!

The Zippiosaur Strikes Again!

Uh-oh! The most scary dinosaur in the world, the **Zippiosaur**, is on the attack again! But don't worry, **Super Bungle** is here to save the day. Look very carefully at these two pictures and see if you can spot **five** small differences between them.

Answers:

1. One of the Zippiosaur's arms has **moved**! 2. The B has **vanished** from Super Bungle's costume! 3. Another rock has **appeared**! 4. A pterodactyl is going the **opposite way** in the background! 5. The sky has **changed colour**!

A Long Stretch

"Look at this, Zippy," says George. "It's very clever..." "**Huh**!" interrupts Zippy. "It doesn't look clever to me!"

"Watch this," says George, stretching the arms of his action figure. "It has special **stretchy** arms and legs!"

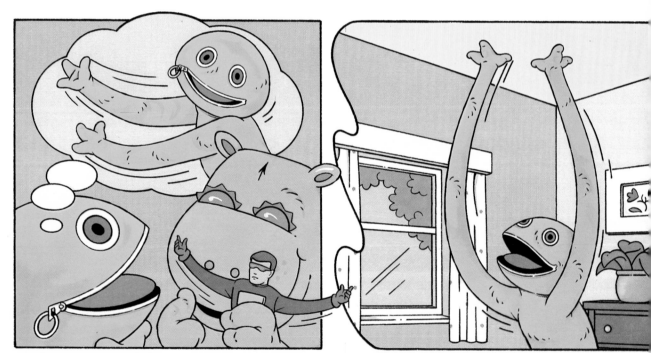

"**Wow**!" gasps Zippy. "That's amazing! I wish I had stretchy arms like that. Just think of all the things I could do..."

Zippy starts daydreaming about having stretchy arms. "This is brilliant!" he laughs. "I can even touch the ceiling!"

"Now, if I hide behind this chair, I'll be able to play a very funny trick on Bungle," Zippy chuckles to himself.

Zippy stretches his arms out towards Bungle. **"Hee, hee**!" laughs Bungle. "Something is tickling me! **Ha, ha, ha**!"

Zippy laughs so much at his joke on Bungle that he tires himself out. "I'll go up to bed for a rest," he thinks.

It is not long before Zippy starts to feel hungry! "I'll stretch my arms downstairs to fetch a banana," he grins.

Zippy soon finds a banana in the fruit bowl downstairs, but his long, stretchy arm gets caught around a table leg!

"**AGGH**! Help! I'm stuck!" cries Zippy, waking up. "Oh, thank goodness for that!" he sighs. "I was only daydreaming."

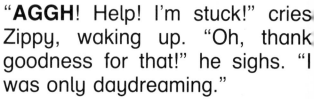

"Now I really do feel hungry," says Zippy. "Would you pass me a banana, please, Bungle?" he asks. "Of course," agrees Bungle.

"I didn't want to get my hand caught around the table leg this time!" explains Zippy. Poor Bungle is very puzzled!

Scaredy-Mouse!

Titch the Mouse thought it would be fun to play a trick on one of his friends. So he put on a **monster mask** and looked around for someone to scare. But, as he passed a mirror, he saw his own reflection and scared **himself**! "Silly me!" he laughed when he realised he had played the trick on himself.

Can you put these pictures into the right order to tell this story?

2

4

Answer: The right order is 3, 2, 4, 1.

Captain Zip's Stars And Rockets Game

Zippy is pretending to be **Captain Zip** of the **Starship Rainbow**. He is on a special mission to visit a strange planet far away in outer space. Now you can join his space crew on their adventures by playing this super